1

Life

On

The Farm.

BY

JOHN C BURT.

4

'Life On The Farm' and a very busy day down of the farm! There was always so much

to do down on
the Farm ..
The Farm was
way out in the
Countryside;
far away from

8

10

the City ... The Farm had a world all it's own ... There were the wide variety of small,

small as small
tractors who
all had the pet
name of Eddy
the Tractor's...
..The Farmer ..

just happened
to like the
name Eddy?
He thought
all his
tractor's were

15

Eddies in their natural temperament; they could on the cold ... morning's be...

hard too start
for the work of
the day? They
all reminded
him of a Man
called Eddy he
knew from the

19

past?

Farmer Richard loved nothing better than too just remain in the warmth of his

Farmhouse! On those cold as cold winter morning's it was hard too leave the house.

22

23

24

25

But Farmer Richard knew that the Farm could not do without him and the Tractor's called

the Eddies?
 So Richard the
Farmer just had
too shake off
the cold and get
into his work on
the Farm?

30

There were of course the minor things on the Farm to do; such as wrangling the ..

newly born;
born not so
long ago chicks;
their Father the
Rooster Mr
Percival helped
as well!

34

35

The Farm of Farmer Richard specialized in producing pumkin's and ..

lots and lots of bright orange, a golden kinda of orange color ..The Farm had won awards for it's Pumkin's !

This has been a snapshot into : 'Life On The Farm?' It's all been about the Tractor's called

the Eddies and
of course the
Farmer
otherwise
known as
Richard the
Farmer !!!

CPSIA information can be obtained
at www.ICGtesting.com
Printed in the USA
BVRC091007110521
607039BV00013B/521

9 781034 905714